JANUARY'S SPARROW

Patricia
Polacco

Philomel Books • Penguin Young Readers Group

With special thanks to Mary McCafferty Douglass
for her research and inspiration.

To the amazing Crosswhite family
and their descendants . . .
with respect and honor
and awe for their courage.

Prologue

I BEEN CALLED MANY THINGS in my time, so's you don't need to know that now. I been owned by white folks for a good part of my life. I can tell you this, they's white folks that have gizzards for hearts. They ain't got no mercy or kindness in them . . . But they's some white folks that do. I don't forget them.

I was sold away from my momma and hauled all the way to Hunter's Bottom in Carroll County, Kentucky, when I wasn't no taller than a porch rail. Sarah and Adam Crosswhite, even tho they was slaves themselves, took me in and held me as they own at the Giltner Plantation. The master wasn't so mean to us in them days, but after his wife died, he took to beatin' me regular.

I was there when Sarah Crosswhite birthed all of her children. John was first, then Ben, then Cyrus, and then came our little sparrow, Sadie. She was all of eight when this story began.

This here is Sadie's story. You hark now. I'm gonna tell it for her, near as I can.

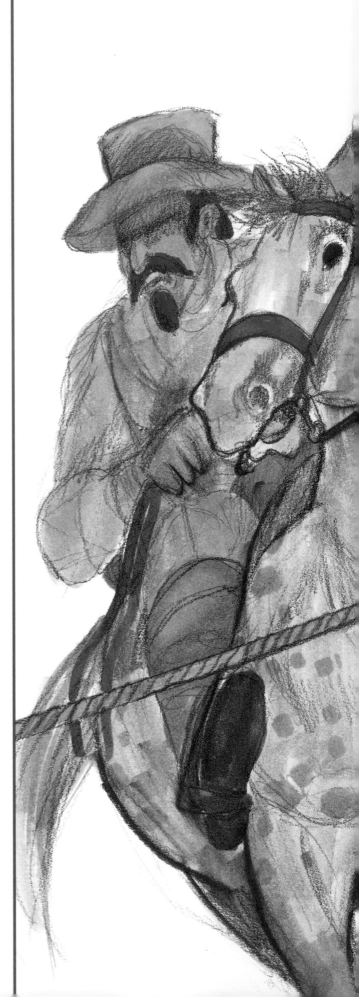

adie, the youngest Crosswhite, shuddered when she saw the paddy rollers thunder into the slave yard on their horses, draggin' a runaway on the end of a rope behind them.

All of the slaves had been ordered to stand at the porch rail that mornin'. They all feared the same thing on that plantation: Master Francis Giltner. Sadie's momma and daddy, Sarah and Adam Crosswhite, and all her brothers gripped at the rail when they saw him rollin' up in his fine carriage, settin' right next to his youngest son, David, and his nephew, Francis Troutman.

The paddy rollers hollered and whooped as they skidded to a dead stop, then hauled off'n they horses and tussled the runaway to his feet.

Sadie almost fell to her knees when she saw who it was they was draggin'. It was January! He had been held so dear to her and her family for as long as she could remember. Her heart fair broke as they smote him and pushed him facedown in the dirt to stake his arms and legs.

Sadie knew January was fixin' to run—he told her hisself only two days before. When he upped and did it, Sadie prayed he'd cross water and make it to Indiana. But now she could see that it wasn't a flick of a sorry dog's tail afore they done caught him and brung him back.

Master Giltner stood over January.

"This here dirt-eatin', lazy no-account known as January Drumm took up and ran. I want you all to see what happens to any brown-skinned devil that runs away from me!" he thundered. Then he motioned to the two men holdin' black snake whips. They was Jimmy Lee and Willie Ford, his paddy rollers and overseers.

First, Ford whipped January cross his back so hard that it cracked the air. With each lash, January's flesh opened up in long red stripes almost to his rib bones. Then while Ford was takin' a dipper of water, Lee commenced to whippin' January in the other direction so's to make his flesh stand up in squares. Lee and Ford whipped and kicked the rags right off from him, but they couldn't make January holler.

Sadie's brother Ben could hardly stand. His knees kept givin' out with each stroke of the whip. Even tho the master had ordered all of them to watch, Ben just hung his head.

When the beatin' was done, Lee and Ford rubbed salt and pepper into January's open back. His skin jerked, quaked, and January twisted and puked up . . . but he never cried out.

Sarah, Sadie's momma, stumbled past January to Master Giltner's carriage and his son, David. Sarah'd held David's momma in her own arms when she was gittin' him born, but his momma died birthin' him. No one knew what to do, so Sarah took that baby home with her. She took him to her own breast even when the other slaves would say, "You lovin' one of the white folks is like a dog lovin' the hickory what beats it." But love him she did and he loved her back. His own daddy hated the sight of him. He blamed that baby for his wife's death. Sarah Crosswhite was the onliest person that loved David. So when her eyes fell on his now, he turned away.

By the time the sun set that evenin' and everyone walked through the slave yard from the fields, January was gone. Each of them looked where he had laid and bowed their heads and touched their hearts.

When Sarah and the children arrived home that night, they all ate in silence. Adam, their daddy, arrived late, carryin' a shovel, his clothes covered in mud 'cause he said he'd been diggin' a grave. They all knew who that grave was for. Sadie burst into tears and ran to the windalight just above her cot and took a small wooden sparrow from the sill.

She held the sparrow next to her cheek as tears burned in her eyes. January had whittled it just for her. She ran her fingers over each of its feathers that he had carved so carefully.

She remembered January whisperin' to her when he put it into her hands. "It's fixin' to fly. And so is I."

She'd known he was gonna run. She'd said nothin' to no one. Now her heart ached at the thought that she hadn't told her momma and daddy. Maybe they could have stopped January. Then he wouldn't have been beaten, and he'd still be here.

She cried herself to sleep.

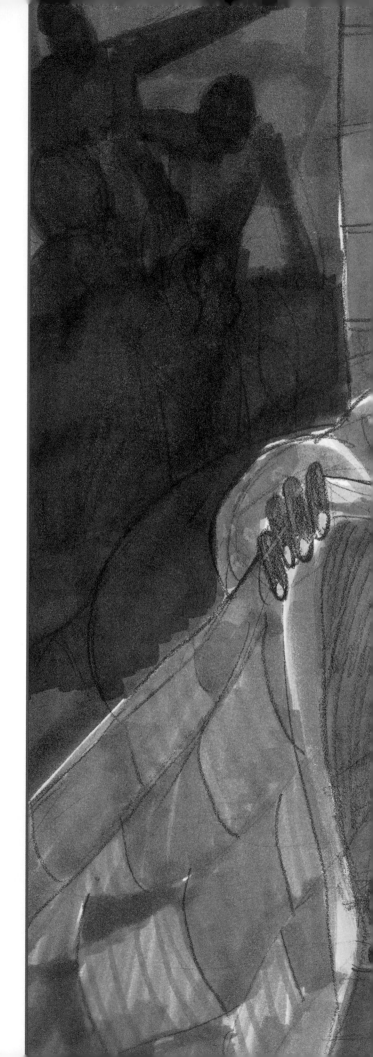

The night was still and black. The next thing Sadie knew, she was shaken awake.

"Wake up, Sadie . . . wake up!" her momma whispered breathlessly.

"But why, Momma . . . what's happenin'?" Sadie moaned. She fussed and cried but got up.

"Get dressed and pack only what you can carry and don't light the lantern," Adam warned. So all of them felt their way around the cabin, pullin' out clothes and crawlin' into 'em. The rest they stuffed into burlap bags. Sadie's heart was racin'.

All of the children and their momma huddled around the door in the darkness.

"Hark now," their daddy whispered. "We is gonna cross water tonight!"

Everyone looked at one another. Sadie just didn't understand. What had happened?

"Now, all of you stay close to me. Thaddeus Quill is comin' to take us to the boat," Adam whispered.

When Thaddeus arrived, they all sneaked out, not makin' a sound. They crossed the slave yard, went by the big house and finally stood near the bottoms. Just as they were about to start into Eliza's woods, Sadie suddenly cried out, "Momma!"

Sarah clapped her hand over Sadie's mouth. "Quiet, girl!" Sarah warned.

"My sparrow . . . January's sparrow . . . I left it on the sill!" Sadie whispered.

Her father knelt in front of her. "Oh, sweet baby, we can't go back for it now. It's too dangerous!" he whispered as he hugged her and started into the woods.

"Why are we leavin' anyway?" Sadie sobbed. She couldn't understand where they were runnin' to and why . . . without her sparrow.

Sarah took Sadie's face in her hands. "They was comin' to fetch the boys in the mornin'. We heard it ourselves. They was gonna be auctioned off.

"Ain't nobody takin' any of my babies," Sarah mumbled.

They all walked in silence through the woods after that—it seemed like hours—until Thaddeus put up his hand. They could hear rushin' waters.

"That's the Ohio," Thaddeus whispered.

"An' that's the water we gonna cross tonight," Adam added.

Sadie's heart was beatin' so hard she could hear it.

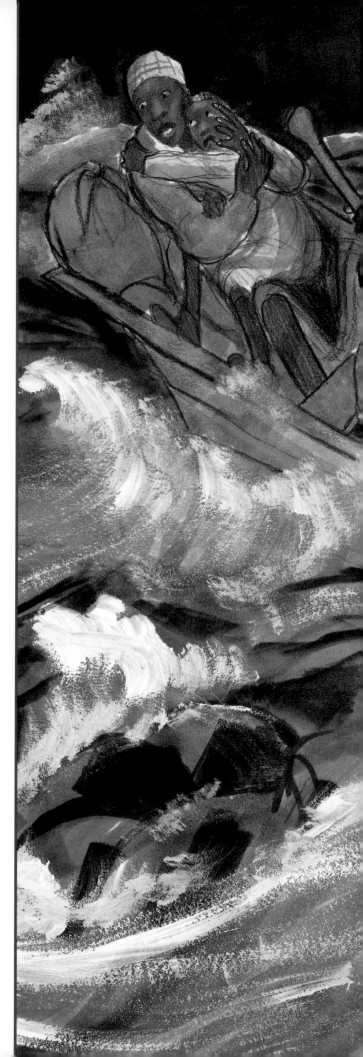

s they came to the bank of the river, they could see a small rowboat near the shore. "I here," a girl's voice called out from the shadow of the boat. "Git in!"

They all crawled into the rockin' boat. The current took the boat right away. The boat girl rowed with her head bowed so's they couldn't see her face. Adam knew about the boat lifters. He knew not to call Sarah and his children by name, so if paddy rollers took to beatin' the girl, she couldn't tell 'em names she never heard. He knew she wouldn't look at any of their faces so's she couldn't tell 'em about faces she done never seen.

The girl took to pullin' them oars with the power of a growed man. Sadie and her brothers caught their breath when the boat leaned way over with the strong current. "Hush now," the girl said. "Sound carries across the water. I done this so many times I know every turnback, bottom rock, and whirlround in this here river . . . so don't none of you fret!"

All of them watched as the shore of Kentucky disappeared into the fog. They all tried to look ahead for the shore of Indiana, where they were headin', but the fog was too thick. The boat pitched and rolled and the water commenced to boil underneath them. Sadie, Ben and Cyrus began to cry. John was tremblin' and clenched his teeth. They all knew that none of them could swim.

"You know they's a line right down the center of
this here river," the rowin' girl called out. "One side
of that line you is owned . . . the other side . . . you
ain't . . . and we crossin' over that line right now!"

They all looked at the water beneath them.

"All the fish on the Kentucky side ain't free . . .
but on the Indiana side they is!" the boat lifter
crowed. "Pretty soon you be as free as them fish!"

The boat turned on itself a few more times, and
then, as fast as the churnin' came, it was gone. They
could make out a little finger of land not too far
ahead. Soon the boat grounded ashore.

"Folks, this here is Indiana, a free state," the
rowin' girl announced.

The Crosswhites tumbled onto the shore.

"Watch for a lantern up on that ridge. They'll take you where you be safe," the rowin' girl whispered. Then, without another word, she back-oared the boat into the river.

The Crosswhites just stood there in the blackness of the night. They all pondered on that girl. She had risked her life for them and probably many others . . . yet they didn't even know her name.

They listened to the sluffin' of her oars till they was no more sound of them.

Adam drew in a deep long breath and sighed. "This here is free air!" he cried out as he fell to his knees in the slap mud.

They knelt there with him, huddled together, all of them takin' gulps of that free air.

You need to haul up this bank," a man's voice called out to them. They all looked up. There was a man holdin' a lantern. Quick as flint, they scrambled up that bluff.

"Stay on my heels next to the fields. Hurry now, we don't got a lot of time before first light. Sometimes slave catchers are fast on the trail of runners. They come right across this here river . . ." he said breathlessly as he scurried along.

Suddenly there were dogs bayin' way off in the distance.

"Oh, Daddy. It's Lee and Ford and Mr. Troutman. They's after us!" John cried between clenched teeth.

They all looked back and quickened their steps. The man covered his lantern and pulled them into a cornfield along a row of stalks. At the end there was a lane. They made their way down the lane and could see in first dawn light the outline of a tall barn. He led them into the barn and helped them climb up into the loft.

Sadie started fever dreamin' as soon as she fell asleep and called out for her momma many times. She had terrible nightmares about bein' caught, watchin' Lee and Ford beat her brothers and her momma and daddy.

They slept all of that day only to set out again as soon as it was dark, travelin' only at night so's not to be seen. And so it was . . . night after night. Adam watched the North Star and followed it to the next safe farm or house on what everybody called the Underground Railroad. Some places were marked with a piece of calico tied to a bush by the front door, while others had pots standin' on the front fence posts. If the pot was standin' right side up, it was safe to come to the barn. If the pot was turned over, it wasn't.

It seemed to Sadie that she and her family had been on the run for days and days. They all had blisters sloughin' off their heel caps and toe tops. Sadie's nightmares seemed to be gettin' worse and worse. But they had to press on, bound for Canada, where they would be safe.

One night they heard dogs off in the distance again. They all packed up and ran till they could taste blood in the back of their throats. Near daybreak they sloshed through a creek after their daddy.

"The dogs can't take up our scent through water," he said breathlessly as he ran behind all of them.

"If them dogs get our scent, then we's done for," Cyrus muttered under his breath.

There were many nights like this, but the Crosswhites kept trackin' through cornfields, climbin' up bluffs, rollin' through muck and mud. Always in the cover of night.

Pretty soon one barn looked like the next. John took to carryin' Sadie pretty regular. But ever northward they walked, holdin' for Canada.

Then one mornin' Sadie was shaken awake by an old dark woman. Sadie sat up. She was sleepin' in a real bed with cool, fresh-smellin' linens on a soft mattress. She didn't even remember gettin' into this bed.

"Baby dear," the woman purred. "Look at this precious child." She touched Sadie's cheek. "We gonna rub lard on your ashy skin and take a crokinoe iron to your hair. We'll fix you up like a shiny new penny."

"Where's my momma?" Sadie asked, pullin' her sheets up to her chin.

"Oh, she right here. Your whole family is. They downstairs at the table eatin' a fine breakfast." The old woman beckoned Sadie to follow her downstairs.

When Sadie got to the kitchen, everyone was at the table. It was groanin' with good food. They was hotcakes, molasses, eggs, bacon and grits, and fresh milk! It was the first time the Crosswhites had sat at a table in so long. Sadie eased into a chair. Then she looked out the winda.

"Momma . . . it's daytime!" She jumped out of her chair, dove under the table and rocked, her arms around her knees. "The paddy rollers will get us . . . the paddy rollers will get us," she chanted.

Her momma pulled Sadie up and into her lap.

The old lady rubbed Sadie's back. "Child, you in Michigan—a free state! They ain't no paddy rollers here. You in Marshall. This town is part of the Underground. We help runaways here . . . that's what we do.

"You can call me Aunt Della. Everybody does," she sang out as she eased Sadie back into her chair. "And this here is Miss Nancy Reid, my neighbor."

Miss Nancy turned from the stove and spooned up eggs and grits for Sadie.

"Are we really safe here?" Sadie asked between bites.

"Safe as newborn lambs!" Miss Reid exclaimed as she poured coffee for Adam and Sarah.

"Why, I heard of Marshall, Michigan," Adam said. It seems he heard from an old friend, Moses Patterson. They'd met on one of Adam's trips to sell tobacco for Master Giltner. Moses used to live in Marshall, Adam was sure of it. Why, Moses told Adam that near two thousand people lived in this town and that sixty of them were Negroes! Moses'd said all the colored folk in town knew each other. And when a stranger come through, they was watched to see if'n they was spies from the South lookin' for runaways.

"Even most white folks here in Marshall don't cotton to keepin' slaves. They dead set against it," Nancy Reid went on to say.

"Now, that don't mean that you can trust all white folks here," Aunt Della warned.

"But we'll show you the ones that you can."

"Oh, Daddy, Momma, can we stay here for a while? I'm so tired of runnin'," Sadie pleaded.

"Canada is the only place we'll be safe. It's still against the law of the land to help runaway slaves," Adam whispered.

"Please, Daddy. I don't think I can walk another step!" Cyrus pleaded.

"Not another step!" Ben and John chimed in.

Just as Adam and Sarah were ponderin', there was a knock at the door and in strode the tallest man that Sadie had ever seen. He was wearin' a stovepipe hat that made him look even taller and was as skinny as a yard pole holdin' up a line of washin'.

"Well, I'll be switched!" Adam Crosswhite threw his arms around the man. "Moses Patterson himself! I don't believe my eyes."

"And I don't believe mine, Adam Crosswhite!" Mr. Patterson just kept shakin' his head. "They told me a new family was here, but I can't believe what I'm seein'."

"Sarah, this here is the very man I been talkin' about." Adam beamed.

"Around here, Adam, I'm called Auction Bell," Mr. Patterson announced, pattin' his hat. "Yessir, I go through town and ring this here bell to announce when they's an auction or for 'won-dos.' "

"What's a won-do?" John asked.

"Do you won-do this . . . or do you won-do that. I tell folks 'bout jobs that need doin'." He laughed.

"There, see, you already got a friend here. I think you folks should stay for a while till you git your bearin's," Aunt Della coaxed.

"Adam, they's other Negro folks here that are runaways. They've been here for a year or two. No harm has come to them," Auction Bell added.

"They's white folks here we trust that will give you work. The children can even go to school and git some book learnin'," Nancy Reid said with a wink.

"Oh, please, Daddy," the children pleaded.

"But if'n you do stay here, you can't never tell white folks that you are runaways," Nancy Reid warned. "Not even a hint!"

"As far as folks will know, you are my cousins from Illinois. You are here to help me out. That's what you say." Aunt Della wagged her finger in each of their faces.

Finally, Adam and Sarah agreed to stay.

"But only for a little while, you hear, just to rest up. At first sign of trouble we is headin' out for Canada," Adam warned.

Sadie watched Auction Bell climb up on a small Indian pony. His legs was so long, and the pony so short, the bottoms of his feet almost touched the ground. Sadie laughed out loud. It was the first time she had laughed since she left the plantation. Mr. Patterson took to ringin' that bell and trotted on down the street.

The Crosswhites stayed right there with Aunt Della. Sarah helped her take in wash and clean houses. Adam went to work at Charles Gorham's mercantile store. He was a trusted friend of Aunt Della, part of the Underground, and he helped runaway slaves regular. John got a job at Ketchum's Mill. Mr. Ingersoll, a young lawyer, got the job for him. Ben, Cyrus and Sadie, for the first time in their lives, were enrolled in school.

It was at school that Sadie learned how far Marshall was from Kentucky. Fact is, it was the first time she had seen a map of the whole country.

"See, this here is Michigan," a girl with a golden mop of hair whispered to Sadie as she pointed at the map. "It's the only state in the union that's shaped like a mitten."

"What's a mitten?" Sadie asked.

"It's a knit glove to keep your hands warm in the snow, silly!" the girl answered.

"I never seen snow," Sadie whispered.

"We get snow that's so deep it reaches all the way up to our second-floor windows. . . . Where are you from, anyway?" the girl asked.

She looked puzzled. Sadie remembered what Aunt Della told her to say. "We're from Illinois," she answered.

"But you get as much snow as we do!" she exclaimed.

"My name is Sadie, Sadie Crosswhite," she blurted out, tryin' to change the subject.

"My name's Polly, Polly Hobart. My daddy is the judge here in Marshall." She grabbed Sadie's hand and took to shakin' it.

After school that day, they walked home together.

"I have three brothers," Sadie told Polly.

"I have two of 'em . . . and ain't they smelly, though."

They both laughed.

From that day on, you almost never saw Polly without Sadie or Sadie without Polly.

One day, when Sadie was visitin' Polly, they was playin' dolls up in Polly's room. Suddenly, as she was holdin' one of the dolls, tears rolled down Sadie's cheeks.

"Sadie, what's wrong?" Polly whispered.

"The only toy I ever had that was as beautiful as this was a whittled sparrow that January made for me, and I don't have it anymore!"

"What happened to it?" Polly asked.

"It got left in the house . . . in Illinois."

"Who's January?" Polly asked.

"He was . . . my eldest brother. Ceptin' he wasn't really. He lived with us and I loved him like one," Sadie said softly.

"What happened to him?" Polly asked.

Sadie finally murmured, "He died, least that's what I think. Daddy dug his grave hisself."

Polly hugged Sadie.

"I just wish I still had that sparrow . . ." Sadie sputtered.

Both them little girls sat on the edge of Polly's bed for the longest time.

"Look! Look, Sadie! It's snowin'!" Polly suddenly sang out.

Both girls ran to the windalight and watched the lacy flakes float down from the sky. Sadie, for the first time, saw snow.

That winter, Sadie got to see for herself how deep snow got in Marshall. Polly taught Sadie and her brothers how to make snowmen and snow angels. Polly took the Crosswhite kids sleddin' down deep hills at Ingersoll's Holler by the mill.

Adam Crosswhite was doin' very well at Mr. Gorham's store, so well that he was soon keepin' records and even had people workin' under him. John was earnin' real good at the mill. Mr. Ingersoll even let him read some of his law books. He had commenced to spark Aunt Della's niece and there was talk that they might marry up.

Ben, Sadie and Cyrus took to book learnin' so good that all three of them were on the honor roll. Life was good for the Crosswhites there in Marshall. Sadie wasn't havin' her nightmares as often and the whole family belonged to a church.

Adam and Sarah, along with the Ingersolls and Gorhams, were part of the Underground, helpin' other folks comin' through Marshall on their way to Canada. But not a day went by that any of them let down their guard.

And then came their fourth spring in Marshall. Adam had moved his family into their very own house two summers before. One evenin', Auction Bell came by to tell Sadie's daddy that they was a stranger in town and that everybody was watchin' him.

That night Sadie had a nightmare that was worse than any of the others. She dreamt that Lee, Ford and Troutman broke down their door and tried to drag them out of their home. She woke up in a cold sweat, then eased herself when she remembered she was safe and it was spring and she was in Marshall.

In the spring, a very special blessin' came upon the Crosswhite house. Sarah birthed a sweet baby girl. Sadie had a new sister!

"I'm gonna name her Frances," Sarah whispered as they all gathered around her. Sadie and her brothers looked at each other in shock.

"But Momma, that's Master Giltner's name, and Mr. Troutman's too. How can you do that?" Ben asked.

"So's none of you will ever fear that name again. From now on you'll think of this here baby girl . . . and know that she was born a free person. In a free state. I want her name to stand for freedom from those two men."

hen one night, there was a knockin' on the door. Mr. Gorham and Mr. Ingersoll came by often, but this night they hurried in. They looked bothered. Adam poured them cups of coffee and chicory. They leaned in to Adam.

"There's talk that slave trackers have been seen as close as Coldwater," Gorham said between sips of coffee.

"They was askin' questions about Negroes travelin' through," Ingersoll added.

"Coldwater is only twelve miles away from here," Adam whispered. He could see Sadie peekin' around the edge of the doorway.

"I heard they captured some runaways in Indiana, near as Goshen," Sarah whispered as she sat down near them.

"Well, as long as there is breath in my body, no one is gonna take any runaways from Marshall!" Gorham said as he stood up and pounded his fist on the table.

"Never!" Ingersoll agreed.

The Crosswhites whispered more with the two men, and after a time, Ingersoll and Gorham left. Sadie and her brothers snuck on up to bed. When Sadie fell into sleep, she had one of her feverish nightmares. The paddy rollers came and got her family and took to beatin' all of them. This time Mr. Troutman and Master Giltner was standin' over 'em. She woke bolt upright in her bed. Sweat was runnin' down her forehead and her heart was beatin' so hard she could hear it. She sat up for the rest of the night and watched for the sun to rise.

That next mornin' at breakfast, Adam gathered his family around him for a meetin'. "You probably heard that paddy rollers has been seen south of here. I want you children to know that I have a plan. If ever anyone comes to this here door and tries to take any of us . . . ever . . . I've made a signal with Auction Bell. You know he's not more'n three doors away, so when I fire a single shot in the air, that's his signal to tell the town. People will come to help us . . . Negroes and white folks will come runnin'. I promise you.

"I don't want any of you to fret. But"—he looked at each of his children—"more than ever, you can't tell nobody that we is runaways. You can't never tell that to no one!"

Soon it was summer in Marshall. There had been no more reports of strangers from the South for some time. The county fair was set up near the stockyards south of town. Sadie put on her best shift to go to the fair with Polly. Aunt Della and Miss Nancy made them a picnic basket so's they could set under the shade of the oaks and eat whenever they felt like.

Sadie and Polly loved the excitement of the fair. Both girls ran from exhibit to exhibit. But Sadie suddenly stopped when they was in front of the hog auction. Auction Bell waved and smiled, but Sadie seemed startled and strangely sad.

When the girls was settin' in the shade of the oak trees, Polly finally spoke. "Sadie, somethin's wrong. You seemed so happy. Now you're not. What's wrong?"

"Polly, what would you say if'n I told you that they is such a place here on earth where they auction off people . . . just like them hogs," Sadie whispered, watchin' a man with a stick poke the pigs into a pen.

"What do you mean, Sadie?" Polly asked.

"They's a place where people stand on auction blocks chained together. White folks bid on them to . . ." Sadie's voice trailed off.

Polly just listened.

"White folks come up to 'em and open their mouths and check their hair. They pull babies out of their mommas' arms. I seen it. It don't matter that them mommas fussed and carried on, they babies is taken and sold off!"

"Sold off?" Polly asked.

"They's a place where Negroes is owned by other people," Sadie said as tears rolled down her cheeks. "I come from such a place, Polly. I'm not from Illinois. I come from Kentucky. My momma and my brothers did too. We is owned by Master Giltner . . . we is slaves . . . we is runaways," Sadie sputtered as she covered her face and sobbed.

"That ain't no bother to me, Sadie. You'll always be my best friend in the whole world," Polly whispered. Then the girls hugged.

"Polly, you can't never tell what I just told you, or the paddy rollers—the slave catchers—will find us."

Polly rested her fingers over Sadie's lips. "I promise. I'll never tell our secret, Sadie."

Then the girls ate their picnic together and spoke no more of it.

As the fall came and went, there were still no more reports of slave catchers. Soon the fourth winter that the Crosswhites spent in Marshall was upon them. Christmas was celebrated with great joy. Then it was early January. Baby Frances was ten months old and gettin' into everythin'!

One day, Ben came runnin' in the front door, stompin' the snow off his feet. "Sadie, look. Someone left you a package on the porch. It has your name on it."

He handed Sadie a small calico bundle tied with twine. There was a note. Sadie untied the package. Everyone gasped. It was January's sparrow! The note just had three words . . .

"I found you."

Sadie's momma dropped to her knees on the kitchen floor. "The paddy rollers and Mr. Troutman has found us. They know where we are!" she cried.

"No, Momma . . . January left it. I just know it. I can feel it in my heart!" Sadie gasped as she held the sparrow close to her cheek.

"Oh, baby," Sarah whispered as she knelt in front of Sadie. "Your daddy put January in his grave hisself. You know that . . . you have to know that," she said as she hugged Sadie. Then she turned to Ben and Cyrus. "Go fetch your father," she hissed.

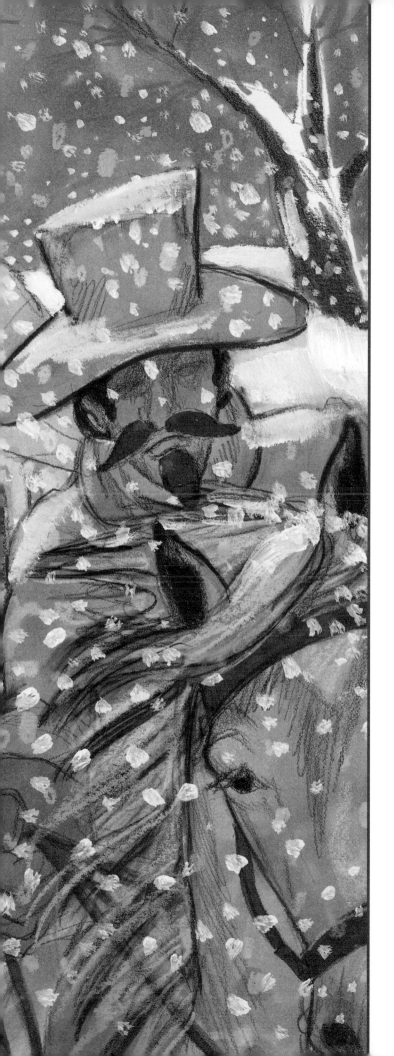

Sadie froze inside. Maybe her momma was right. Her father'd warned her not to tell anyone about where they'd come from, and she'd told Polly. Maybe Polly told someone without meanin' any harm. Oh, maybe this was all Sadie's fault!

When Cyrus and Ben came back with John and their father, Mr. Gorham and Mr. Ingersoll was with them. Sarah told them what happened and showed them January's sparrow. Gorham spoke first. "The only stranger here in town lately was a lawyer lookin' to open his practice here. He told me he was an abolitionist. Of course I told him nothin'. About anyone!"

Mr. Ingersoll sat in a heap at the kitchen table, rubbin' his chin.

"Do you remember what his name was?" Adam asked Gorham, fearin' what he might hear.

"Yes, his name was Francis Troutman," Gorham answered.

"Troutman! My lord, I should have told you the names of the people that would be lookin' for us. I guess I never did. . . ." Adam's voice trailed off.

Sadie and her brothers grabbed on to each other and rocked with fear. Adam paced back and forth.

"What we gonna do?" Sarah wailed.

"There's not a Negro, or white man for that matter, in this here town that is gonna give you up to them!" Ingersoll said sternly.

"Wait a minute. Wait a minute," Gorham broke in. "He left town this afternoon. He wouldn't have left if he thought he had found you!"

Sarah reared up and snatched the sparrow out of Sadie's hands. "But Sadie's sparrow . . . Sadie's sparrow," she wailed as she shook it in each of their faces. "Someone knows exactly who we are . . . and where we are!"

For the next two weeks folks in Marshall was watchful. But no one came into town that wasn't known to them. Folks started feelin' easier.

It was four o'clock in the mornin', January twenty-seventh, eighteen hundred forty-seven, when Adam Crosswhite was jarred awake by a fierce poundin' at his front door. Thinkin' it might be Mr. Gorham, he opened the door. Three men pushed past the door so hard that it almost wrenched clean off'n its hinges.

It was Francis Troutman, Willie Ford and Jimmy Lee!

Lee seized Adam and tried to force him out the front door into a waitin' wagon. David Giltner, the master's son, was drivin'!

But Adam broke free and raced upstairs, shoutin' for his family to hide. The three was right behind him, but he barricaded his bedroom door, threw open his winda and fired a single shot into the air.

"They here!" Adam yelled. "They here to take us away!" He hoped Auction Bell heard. Adam could see lights in the windas up his street just as the three men broke down his door and seized him. As they dragged him down the stairs, Adam could hear Auction Bell ring down the streets, already hollerin' for help.

Sadie and her brothers had hidden in the attic eaves, but one by one Lee and Ford reached in and grabbed 'em out. Sadie started prayin'.

"Dear God, turn me into a sparrow and let me fly far, far away from here . . . Dear God, turn me into a sparrow and let me fly far, far away from here," she chanted.

Then she felt a hand grab her by the hair and drag her down the stairs, her back bumpin' each step and bruisin' all the way down. Lee and Ford flung all of the Crosswhites in a heap on the kitchen floor, then tried to force them all to their feet and out the door into the waitin' wagon.

"It's freezin' out there. My children need their coats and boots," Sarah pleaded. She pulled her children around her. Then her eyes fell on David Giltner. He was just standin' there in the kitchen.

"David . . . you!" she whispered.

He hardened his gaze and didn't look away. "I am here representing the interests of my father, and we are within our rights to take you all back to Kentucky!" he barked.

Sarah came close to his face. "My milk made your bones, boy!" she whispered through clenched teeth. "I held you at my breast and raised you up as my very own . . . and now you can do me like this?" Tears filled her eyes. "Do you think your daddy finally gonna love you for doin' this?" she hissed.

David Giltner looked away and went out to the wagon.

Auction Bell kept ringin'. A crowd started gatherin' outside of the Crosswhite house. People both white and colored started screamin' down the street with sticks, hammers, torches and clubs. They was riled up and shoutin' and shakin' their fists. Some of the men even dropped their coats in that bitter cold and were fixin' to fight.

"You ain't takin' these Crosswhites anywhere!" they yelled. They surged forward, shook their fists and pounded on the outside of the Crosswhite house.

They was comin' from every direction! Even Lee and Ford looked scared.

That's when Francis Troutman went outside, drew his revolver and pointed it at the crowd.

"Stand back . . . stand back, I say!" he ordered as he spun around, pointin' the gun at them. The crowd pulled back.

The deputy sheriff pushed his way from the back of the crowd and stood with Troutman, glowerin' at the crowd. "These here men," he announced over the din of the mob, "have the right, under the law, to reclaim their property!"

The crowd roared. "Property! People ain't nobody's property," a voice called out.

The deputy tried to shout over the protests. "These here Negroes are the Giltners' property. It's the law! Now, all of you stand down!" he barked.

Troutman holstered his pistol and crossed his arms defiantly outside the front door.

In the house, Jimmy Lee lurched at Sarah Crosswhite and latched baby Frances by her ankles. "We're takin' 'em . . . and none of you can stop us. That's the law!" Lee growled.

Sarah screamed and fell back, still holdin' her baby. Lee pulled at both of them as Sarah skidded on the floorboards with her heels. Suddenly the crowd parted and Gorham and Ingersoll came burstin' through and into the house. They wrestled the baby away from Lee.

"This child was born in a free state. She is a freeborn citizen of Marshall and you cannot take her!" Gorham shouted.

He and Ingersoll forced the Kentucky four out of the Crosswhites' kitchen and shoved them out the front door. Then Gorham and Ingersoll stood with their backs to the door, the Crosswhites safe inside.

Gorham leaned into Francis Troutman's face. "Like I said, you ain't takin' these people anywhere. . . ."

The crowd surrounded the four and leaned toward them, crowdin' them in.

Francis Troutman straightened his coat and tried to catch his composure. "I want all of your names!" He took a pad from his pocket. "And I am takin' these names to your magistrate, demandin' that he order your arrest. You are all breakin' the law," he thundered over the grumblin' crowd.

The crowd suddenly grew quiet for a long moment. Then a Negro stepped forward.

"I is Planter Morse," he said.

"I'm James Smith," another said.

"I'm C. W. Hackett," still another said.

"And I am Charles Berger."

"I'm Willie Parker." One after another stepped up and wagged their heads, mockin' Troutman.

Then Ingersoll, Hurd, Easterly and even Dr. Comstock, all white men, gave their names.

"And I am Charles Gorham . . . spelled G-O-R-H-A-M. Be sure you put it in capital letters!" Gorham said triumphantly.

The crowd roared its approval and started to push at each of the Kentucky men. They jostled them about like bouncin' balls, laughin' when one lost his balance and fell.

Even the deputy was full of fear. He drew his gun and fired into the air. The crowd pulled back. He turned full circle, aimin' his pistol at everyone. "The fact remains," he said breathlessly, "that these here Crosswhites are fugitive slaves." He whirled around as the crowd roared. "Under the Fugitive Slave Act of 1793, these men have the legal right to take back these here slaves." He turned around. "To their rightful owner."

The crowd roared at him. He lifted his pistol at them again. "Their rightful owner . . . Mr. Francis Giltner!" the deputy shouted.

The crowd seemed to pull back. "What if'n he's right," a voice called out. Then the crowd just stood there. No one seemed to know what to do next.

Then a lone voice called from among them.

"If you let these men take this family back to Kentucky, they'll be whipped and tortured and left for dead. Like I was . . ."

A young Negro stepped forward and stood in front of the Crosswhites' door, facin' the crowd.

"This is what will happen to them," he said as he removed his overcoat and then his shirt. In the bitter cold, steam rose up off his scarred skin. He put out his arms and slowly turned his back to the crowd.

All that stood there was stunned to silence.

"You!" Ford hissed as he stared at the young man. "Boy, you should be dead!"

"We shoulda lynched ya," Lee grumbled as he spat at the young man's feet.

"January, January, I knew you was alive!" Sadie called out as soon as she saw his face.

She took his hand and pulled him into the kitchen, where all of the Crosswhites wept and hugged him.

"You've come to us . . . praise God . . . you've come home to us," Adam cried as he held January's face in his hands.

Outside the front door, the crowd was louder and angrier than ever. January gave them the reason to press into the Kentucky four like a Michigan tornado. They pushed at them, tugged at them and yelled at them.

When Mr. Gorham put up his hand, the crowd listened.

"This is a matter for Judge Hobart," he said.

"Judge Hobart! Judge Hobart!" the crowd roared and they pressed the Kentucky four right up off their feet. Then they herded them down the street like cattle . . . right down to the courthouse.

All of the Crosswhites shed tears of happiness, even knowin' their life here in Marshall was over now that Giltner knew where they was. I wasn't safe either, now that they knew I—January—was alive. We all would have to set out for Canada.

Within the hour we had almost finished packin' what we could when Mr. Ingersoll arrived in his wagon to take us to Jackson to catch the train headin' for Detroit. He came all out of breath and covered with snow, but he was smilin' so broadly, everyone wondered why.

"Judge Hobart just jailed Lee, Ford, Giltner and Troutman for attemptin' to kidnap you, and for assault!" he said, laughin' and slappin' his knee.

Adam and Sarah looked at each other, puzzled.

"His clerk said to tell you all that he is goin' to hold them there in jail for the next two days. That should give you enough time to get to Canada before they can catch up to you!" Ingersoll trumpeted.

Sadie smiled to herself. She knew exactly why Judge Hobart kept them there. Polly . . . Polly must have told her father the secret. "Thank you, Polly," Sadie whispered to herself, and then smiled. But tears filled her eyes. There would be no time to say good-bye to Polly, her best friend.

I guess some secrets is meant to be kept and some ain't. Now, I said at the beginnin' that this here was Sadie's story, but I guess it's as much mine too.

That day back in Kentucky, when I was beat so bad and left staked out for dead—that night, Adam came for me. He carried me hisself into the woods and hid me with Thaddeus Quill. Oh, he dug my grave all right, but he put nothin' but field rocks in it. He marked it so the master and the paddy rollers would never look for me again. When the Crosswhites left, Thaddeus brung me Sadie's sparrow. He knew how much she loved it, and he knew that one day I'd find her and give it back to her. So I carried that sparrow for four years. All the while hopin' to find the only family I ever knowed.

I guess I repaid Adam Crosswhite for savin' my sorry life by bein' there early that mornin' when the paddy rollers was tryin' to take him and his family back to Kentucky. Now we's a family again. We left Marshall knowin' there was talk of freein' the slaves and even talk of war with the South. So's even tho we was all so sad to leave, we was full of hope too.

After we was gone, Francis Troutman did come back to Marshall and took all of them men that gave up their names to court. Because of the slave act, they was forced to pay. But in 1860 Abraham Lincoln was elected president, and in the middle of the war between the North and the South—the Civil War—he gave all slaves their freedom.

Now, I knows all the history books will say that the war was started with the first shot fired at Fort Sumter, but for us—and all the citizens of Marshall, Michigan—the real first shot was fired that mornin' in January 1847 by Adam Crosswhite.

Leastwise, that's what we believe . . .

After the Civil War, the Crosswhites returned to Marshall. They lived out their lives both there and in nearby Battle Creek in freedom and peace. Sadie remained a lifelong friend of Polly Hobart Chancellor and continued to be a devoted sister to her beloved January Drumm.

Upon January's death and shortly before her own, Sadie Crosswhite-Crosby held her most prized possession bundled in a faded piece of worn calico. Inside was a small carved sparrow. She took it to her fireplace and committed it to the flames.

Then she spoke these last words to her only son: "It's fixin' to fly . . . and so is I."

The dialect for this book is a modified dialect derived from entries in *Unchained Memories: Readings from the Slave Narratives*, an adaptation of the original HBO documentary of the same name, published in 2003 by Little, Brown & Company.

PATRICIA LEE GAUCH, EDITOR
PHILOMEL BOOKS
A division of Penguin Young Readers Group.
Published by The Penguin Group. Penguin Group (USA) Inc., 375 Hudson Street, New York, NY 10014, U.S.A. Penguin Group (Canada), 90 Eglinton Avenue East, Suite 700, Toronto, Ontario M4P 2Y3, Canada (a division of Pearson Penguin Canada Inc.). Penguin Books Ltd, 80 Strand, London WC2R 0RL, England. Penguin Ireland, 25 St. Stephen's Green, Dublin 2, Ireland (a division of Penguin Books Ltd). Penguin Group (Australia), 250 Camberwell Road, Camberwell, Victoria 3124, Australia (a division of Pearson Australia Group Pty Ltd). Penguin Books India Pvt Ltd, 11 Community Centre, Panchsheel Park, New Delhi - 110 017, India. Penguin Group (NZ), 67 Apollo Drive, Rosedale, North Shore 0632, New Zealand (a division of Pearson New Zealand Ltd). Penguin Books (South Africa) (Pty) Ltd, 24 Sturdee Avenue, Rosebank, Johannesburg 2196, South Africa.
Penguin Books Ltd, Registered Offices: 80 Strand, London WC2R 0RL, England.

Published simultaneously in Canada. Manufactured in China by South China Printing Co. Ltd. Text set in 16-point Adobe Jenson.
The illustrations are rendered in pencils and markers.

Design by Semadar Megged.

Library of Congress Cataloging-in-Publication Data
Polacco, Patricia. January's sparrow / Patricia Polacco. p. cm. Summary: After a fellow slave is beaten to death, Sadie and her family flee the plantation for freedom through the Underground Railroad. 1. Underground Railroad—Juvenile fiction. [1. Underground Railroad—Fiction. 2. Slavery—Fiction. 3. Fugitive slaves—Fiction. 4. Freedom—Fiction. 5. Family life—Fiction. 6. African Americans—Fiction.] I. Title. PZ7.P75186Jan 2009 [Fic]—dc22 2008052726
ISBN 978-0-399-25077-4
9 10